ELOISE AND BROTHERS

These charming and amusing stories about Mervyn Mouse are written in rhyme for younger children. When Mervyn loses his tail, his mother replaces it with a rubber band and his adventures begin. In Mervyn Swims the Channel his tail causes Mervyn a lot of trouble until he is rescued by some French mice.

two tales of
Mervyn Mouse

by SYLVIA CRECHE

designed and illustrated
by ROGER TWINN

Ladybird Books Loughborough

Mervyn was a country mouse
Who lived on Old Pete's farm.
He nibbled at the corn all day,
And caused a lot of harm.

So one day, whilst feeding,
Young Mervyn met his fate.
The combine sliced his tail clean off
And didn't stop to wait.

"Oh! Wheatgerms!" stammered Mervyn,
Staring at his stump.
Then he shook his little fist
And said, "You silly chump!"

Looking red and angry,
He ran to show his mother.
He asked her what he ought to do
And if he'd grow another.

Mother stood and listened,
Then started to explain
That once a mouse had lost its tail,
It would not grow again.

"I feel completely naked,"
Her son began to wail.
"How can I face the rest of life
With half an inch of tail?"

Kissing him upon the nose,
His mother took his hand.
Then standing Mervyn on a chair,
She fetched a rubber band.

She tied it to his little stump
And, when her task was done,
She sent him out to show his friends,
Who thought it rather fun.

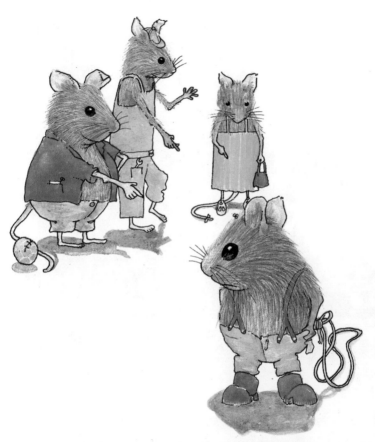

"Please don't point," cried Mervyn,
"I mind that very much.
Those who wish to take a look
Must promise not to touch."

"I promise!" shouted Harry.
"I think it's very nice."
Then taking hold of Mervyn's tail,
He pinged him with it twice.

Skinny Bill and Lucy Mouse
Began to do the same,
Calling all the other mice
To join their latest game.

"Go away!" yelled Mervyn,
As they gathered in a ring.
"Keep your fat hands to yourselves,
My tail's not meant to ping!"

Through the day they teased him,
Their point became quite clear.
So Mervyn said, "I've had enough.
I'm getting out of here!"

"Please don't go," begged Mother.
"It's growing very late."
But Mervyn grabbed his little bag
And ran out through the gate.

All that night he travelled.
He had to get away
To see his uncle up in town,
To ask if he could stay.

Uncle owned a mousehole
At a very smart hotel.
He fed upon the finest food
And lived extremely well.

Mervyn told his uncle
Of how he'd lost his tail,
And how he travelled from the farm
Through valley, hill and dale.

Stroking Mervyn's furry head,
He sat him on his knee.
He bounced his nephew up and down
And gave him milky tea.

"You go back to Old Pete's farm,
And face them proud and tall.
A rubber tail is best by far
Than nothing there at all."

"Being teased is awful.
It isn't any fun.
Can't I drop them all a line,
Or phone them one by one?"

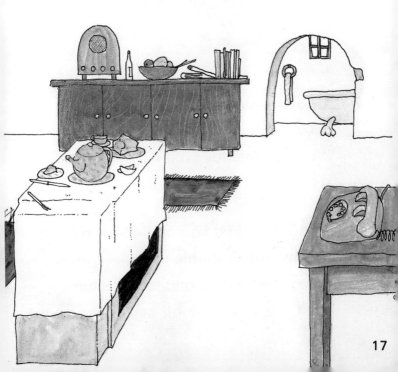

"Calm yourself," said Uncle.
"You're getting in a stew.
You cannot stay with me, dear boy,
There's nothing I can do.

"You must find courage, Mervyn.
Throw out your little chest,
Laugh with them and join the fun
And you will come off best."

Mervyn stayed there all that night,
Sharing Uncle's bed.
He thought about his talk with him
And all the things he'd said.

And so it was next morning,
He left his uncle's house,
Homeward bound for Old Pete's farm,
A wiser little mouse.

Happily, he waved goodbye,
Though this is not the end,
For more adventures lie in wait,
Just around the bend . . .

Mervyn
swims the Channel

"I'll swim the English Channel,"
Mervyn told the others.
"If you're with me, raise your hands
And go and tell your mothers."

"You must be mad!" cried Henry.
"You cannot swim a length.
The Channel's more than twenty miles,
You'd never have the strength."

"Stop him!" pleaded Lucy.
"He'll make himself so ill.
He's very prone to cold you know
And bound to catch a chill."

"None-the-less," said Mervyn,
"I'm swimming to Calais.
You can follow in the boat
And shout, 'Hip, hip, hooray'!"

"Very well," they all agreed,
Chewing on their clover.
"We'll go and ask our mothers now,
And see you off from Dover."

So it was, by twelve midday,
They reached their destination.
Mervyn waved the train goodbye
And danced across the station.

Marching proudly through the town,
They headed for the beach.
Henry waved his favourite flag
And Mervyn gave a speech . . .

. . . "Fellow mice!" he shouted,

"I can only do my best.

So wish me luck; goodbye, my friends.

Now has come the test . . ."

"I will grease you," Lucy said.
"I've brought a pound of lard.
You mustn't catch a cold, my dear.
We mice are none too hard."

Mervyn gave a mighty screech
And dived straight in the ocean.
He never heard her frantic cries
Of love and deep devotion.

"Stop him!" shouted Skinny Bill.
"We haven't planned his route.
Apart from which, he cannot swim
In mac and welly boots."

Lucy grabbed at Mervyn's tail
And swung him back to land.
Then she greased him carefully,
While Henry held his hand.

"Forward lad!" said Henry.

"We'll follow on by boat.

Keep your chin up from your chest

And try to stay afloat."

33

Everyone began to cheer,
As Mervyn took the plunge.
He was bobbing in the water
Like a greasy little sponge.

Behind him came the others
But their pace was very slow.
Skinny Bill turned vivid green
And Lucy couldn't row!

"Will he sink?" she whispered.
"I fear he's overweight.
We should have put him on a diet
But now it's all too late."

Mervyn swam on bravely.
The skies grew dark and black.
Thunder boomed and raindrops fell,
He wished he'd worn his mac.

Suddenly, without ado,
A *monster* grabbed his tail.
Then with Mervyn right behind,
Across the sea did sail.

"Put me down!" screamed Mervyn,
But the speedboat did not shudder.
It didn't know a little mouse
Was dangling from its rudder.

The boat went even faster,
Fifty knots at least.
Mervyn threw himself about
And called it 'fiery beast'.

When at last he landed
On Calais' golden shore,
He felt quite hot and *very* cross,
And in the mood for war.

"Help me!" Mervyn shouted,
"Get me down from here . . .
SOMEONE COME AND RESCUE ME,
I'm hanging from the rear."

"Hello," said a little voice,
"Why are you so mad?
Don't you like the Continent?
It's really not so bad."

41

Mervyn paused in wonder,
He couldn't even speak.
He stared into her bright pink eyes
And turned a trifle weak.

"I am Eloise," she said.
"Tell me who you are.
Are you here on holiday?
Have you travelled far?"

"I'm Mervyn Mouse," he stammered.
"I tried to swim the Channel.
Please excuse my dreadful state,
I must look like a flannel."

"I'll go and fetch my brothers.
Our house is on the rock.
Would you like a cup of tea?
It's very good for shock."

Eloise returned with tea,
Along with seven brothers,
Jac and Paul and Big Pierre
(She did not name the others).

"Now, Monsieur," said Big Pierre.
"I will climb on deck,
Free your little rubber tail
And tie it round your neck!"

"Naughty boy!" cried Eloise.
"You mustn't be so rude.
Rescue poor Monsieur at once,
He's freezing in the nude."

They listened most politely
To Mervyn's long lost cause.
He chatted on about himself
Without a moment's pause.

"English mouse," sighed Big Pierre,
"Never give up hope.
Swim on back to Dover.
I'm certain you can cope."

So it was that afternoon
He dived back in the sea.
The French mice followed in a boat,
All armed with flasks of tea.

Mervyn swam for miles and miles,
Until by five to seven,
He sighted Dover's tall, white cliffs
Reaching up to heaven.

. . . Meanwhile, in the rowing boat,
Sick and half asleep,
Skinny Bill saw Mervyn's head
And gave a mighty leap !

"Look out, English!" yelled the French.
"Our boats are going to crash."
The warning came too late for all.
The only sound was SPLASH!

Mervyn, having reached the shore,
Laughed until he cried,
As one by one they drifted in,
Assisted by the tide.

Then everyone apologised.
And that was rather nice.
The English hugged their hero,
But *he* thanked those *other* mice.

Au revoir (until the next time)

THE FAMILY AND FRIENDS